MAX AND RUBY'S
·MIDAS·

ANOTHER GREEK MYTH

ROSEMARY WELLS

DIAL BOOKS FOR YOUNG READERS NEW YORK

⋆ *For Amy and Cynthia Glidden* ⋆

Published by Dial Books for Young Readers
A Division of Penguin Books USA Inc.
375 Hudson Street
New York, New York 10014

Typography by Jane Byers Bierhorst
Printed in the U.S.A.
First Edition
3 5 7 9 10 8 6 4 2

Library of Congress Cataloging in Publication Data
Wells, Rosemary.
Max and Ruby's Midas : another Greek myth / Rosemary Wells.
p. cm.
Summary: Ruby tries to stop her younger brother Max from eating
so many sweets by reading him an altered
version of the story of King Midas.
ISBN 0-8037-1782-2.—ISBN 0-8037-1783-0 (lib. bdg.)
[1. Food habits—Fiction. 2. Brothers and sisters—Fiction.
3. Rabbits—Fiction.] I. Title. II. Title: Midas.
PZ7.W46843Mars 1995 [E]—dc20 94-11181 CIP AC

The artwork for each picture is an
ink drawing with watercolor painting.

"Hello, Beautiful!" whispered Max.

“I see you and I hear you, Max,”
said Max’s sister, Ruby.

"And I see those lumps and bumps in your pajamas!"

"Back they go, Max," said Ruby. "One more of these and you'll turn into a cupcake."

"Now, Max," said Ruby. "I am going to read you a bedtime story about someone whose sweet tooth got out of control. Are you ready, Max?"

"Yes!" said Max.

"Then listen up," said Ruby.

Once upon a time in Ancient Greece there was a little prince named Midas who hated his fruits and vegetables. Midas spent a lot of time in his mother's kitchen glaring at her olive loaves. He kept trying to turn them into sweets by developing laser-beam eyes.

One morning Midas's mother put prune whip on his melon.
"Oh, no," growled Midas.
"You must eat a good breakfast, my little pomegranate,"
said his mother. "Then you will grow big and strong."

Midas decided to try something he had never done before. As he laser-beamed his eyes, he whispered the words "hot fudge sundae!" at the prune whip. It worked beyond his wildest dreams.

Midas's breakfast was transformed into a table of ice cream delights. Unfortunately his mother's hand had gotten in the way of the laser-beam. She became a cherry float.

The ice cream was delicious
and took until lunchtime to eat.

Midas's father called him into the fountain room for lunch. "Spinach soup is full of vitamins, Son!" said Midas's dad. Midas whispered the words "pistachio pop!" at the soup, but just as he lasered his eyes at the spoon of green liquid, he sneezed and nicked his father on the sleeve.

The spinach soup speedily turned into a pistachio pop, but Midas's father was locked into the rubbery swirls of a lime Jell-O surprise.

At four o'clock Midas's sister, Athena, called him
for an afternoon snack.

She had made him a freshly baked carrot muffin. Aiming carefully, Midas zinged his laser eyes at the muffin. But by accident he hiccuped, missed the muffin, and ticked Athena on a whisker.

Athena became a slice of birthday cake.
Midas pleaded for her to come back, but no amount of persuading could coax his sister out from the layers.

"What have I done?" moaned Midas.

He looked high and low for his family, but all he could find was melted ice cream and sagging Jell-O.

Midas sped to the top step of the escalarium. Using every volt in his body, he sent his lasers scooting down the bannister, up the drainpipes, and into every corner of every room in the house.

"Mom! Dad! Athena!" he shouted. "Come back!"

After a moment Midas heard tinkling laughter from the kitchen.

"Dinnertime!" said Midas's mother.
"And we have your favorite dessert for you!"
said Midas's father.

“Hot fudge sundae!” Athena sang out.
“Oh, no,” said Midas.

“Broccoli!” he whispered.

Ruby closed the book.
"Midas had too much of a good thing, didn't he, Max?" asked Ruby.
But Max didn't answer.
"Good night, Max," said Ruby.

“Good night, Beautiful!” said Max.

Healthy Eating

Grains

Nancy Dickmann

Heinemann Library
Chicago, Illinois

www.heinemannraintree.com
Visit our website to find out more information about Heinemann-Raintree books.

To order:

Phone 888-454-2279

Visit www.heinemannraintree.com to browse our catalog and order online.

an imprint of Capstone Global Library, LLC
Chicago, Illinois

Edited by Siân Smith, Nancy Dickmann, and Rebecca Rissman
Designed by Joanna Hinton-Malivoire
Original Illustrations © Capstone Global Library Ltd 2010
Illustrated by Tony Wilson
Picture research by Elizabeth Alexander
Production by Victoria Fitzgerald
Originated by Capstone Global Library Ltd
Printed and bound in China by South China Printing Company Ltd

ISBN 978-1-4329-3980-9
14 13 12 11 10
10 9 8 7 6 5 4 3 2 1

Library of Congress Cataloging-in-Publication Data

Dickmann, Nancy.
Grains / Nancy Dickmann.
p. cm. -- (Healthy eating)
Includes bibliographical references and index.
ISBN 978-1-4329-3980-9 (hc) -- ISBN 978-1-4329-3987-8 (pb) 1. Grain in human nutrition--Juvenile literature. I. Title.
QP144.G73D53 2011
613.2--dc22

2009045481

Acknowledgements
We would like to thank the following for permission to reproduce photographs: Capstone Publishers p.**22** (© Karon Dubke); Corbis p.**21** (© Roy McMahon); Getty Images pp.**8** (White Rock/DAJ), **12** (Tanya Constantine/Photographer's Choice), **17** (Tara Moore/Taxi); Photolibrary pp.**5** (Emely/Cultura), **6** (Gilles Rouget/Photononstop); Shutterstock pp.**4**, **23 bottom** (© Elena Elisseeva), **7 main** (© MarFot), **7 inset** (© Petrenko Andriy), **9** (© iwka), **10** (© Morgan Lane Photography), **11** (© Victoria Visuals), **13**, **23 top** (© Monkey Business Images), **14** (© 6493866629), **15** (© Mikus, Jo.), **16** (© Nic Neish) **18** (© Flashon Studio), **20** (© paulaphoto); USDA Center for Nutrition Policy and Promotion p.**19**.

Front cover photograph of grains reproduced with permission of © Capstone Publishers (Karon Dubke). Back cover photograph reproduced with permission of Corbis (© Roy McMahon).

We would like to thank Dr Sarah Schenker for her invaluable help in the preparation of this book.

Every effort has been made to contact copyright holders of material reproduced in this book. Any omissions will be rectified in subsequent printings if notice is given to the publishers.

Contents

What Are Grains?

Grains are the seeds from some plants.

Eating grains can keep us healthy.

Wheat and rice are grains.

Oats are grains.

Food from Grains

We cook some grains before eating.

We make some grains into flour.

Bread and pasta are made from flour.

Some tortillas are made from flour.

How Grains Help Us

Eating grains gives you energy.

You need energy to work and play.

Some foods are made with part of the grain.

Some foods are made with the whole grain.

Eating whole grains helps your body fight illness.

Eating whole grains helps keep your heart healthy.

Healthy Eating

We need to eat different kinds of food each day.

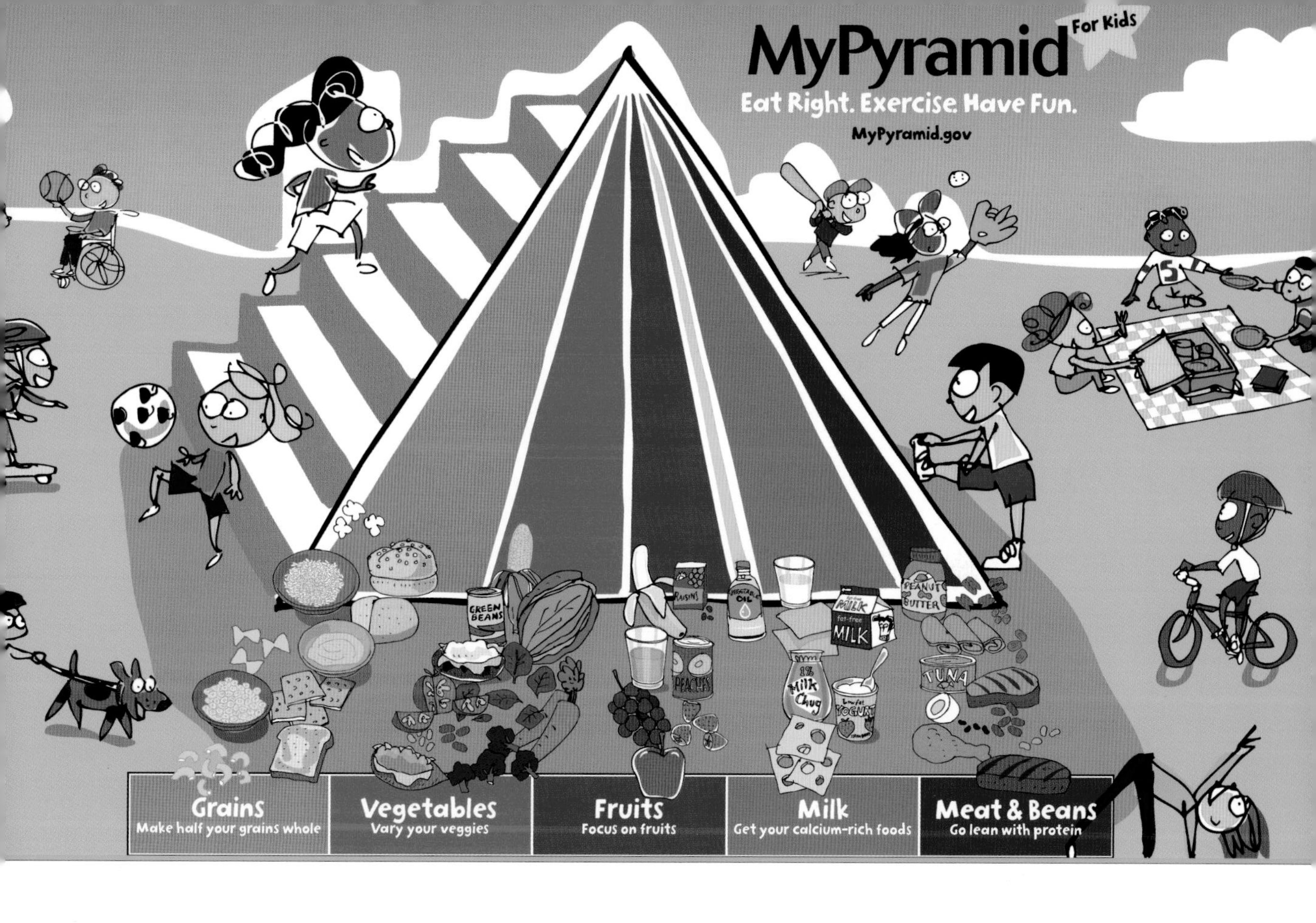

The food pyramid tells us to eat foods from each food group.

We eat grains to stay healthy.

We eat grains because they taste good!

Find the Grains

Here is a healthy dinner. Can you find a food made from grains?

Answer on page 24

Picture Glossary

energy the power to do something. We need energy when we work or play.

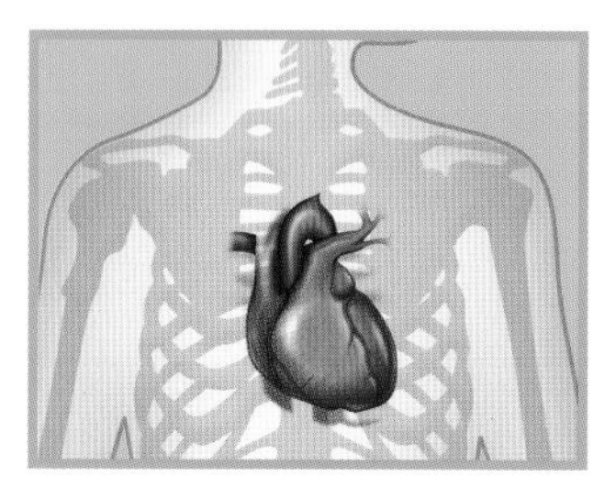

heart part of your body inside your chest. Your heart pushes blood around your body.

seed plants make seeds. Seeds grow into new plants. We can eat some seeds.

Index

Answer to quiz on page 22: The bread is made from grains.

Notes for parents and teachers

Before reading

Explain that we need to eat a range of different foods to stay healthy. Splitting foods into different groups can help us understand how much food we should eat from each group. Show the grains section of the food pyramid on page 19. Grains are seeds from plants. Eating grains gives us energy.

After reading

- Play "Spot the grains." Take children around a supermarket in small groups and ask them to draw or record all the grains they see. Alternatively, hold up pictures of different types of food and ask the children twhether they think grains are being shown in each picture.
- Discuss the difference between foods made with whole grain (literally the entire grain kernel) such as whole wheat bread, and foods where part of the grain has been removed, such as white flour, white bread, and white rice. Explain that whole grain foods are much better for us. Bring in three different types of whole wheat bread (checking that no children have gluten or nut allergies). Conduct a taste test to see which kind of bread is the favorite.
- Help the children to each design a healthy lunch (or lunch box). Discuss the sorts of things that might go into a healthy lunch and the importance of including a range of different types of food. What grains are they going to include? The lunches could be drawn on paper plates and displayed along with an illustrated drink for each meal.